Brigitte Weninger

Good-Bye, Daddy!

Illustrated by Alan Marks

A Michael Neugebauer Book
North-South Books / New York / London

When Tom came back home with Daddy, he sat on the floor in the middle of the hall, folded his arms, and scowled.

Daddy took off Tom's jacket and scarf. Then he smiled and picked a blade of grass out of Tom's hair—but Tom just scowled harder.

Daddy went to talk to Tom's mother in the kitchen, and Tom got up and hid behind the coats hanging in the hallway.

Then Daddy had to go.

He called to Tom, but Tom didn't answer, and he didn't come out.

So Daddy had to leave without his good-bye hug.

Mother found where Tom was hiding. She tried to cheer him up, but he shouted and stamped and didn't want to cheer up.

Then he ran to his room, flopped onto his bed, and started to cry.

Mother sat on his bed and patted him on the back.
Then she took his teddy bear off the shelf, put it in Tom's arms,
and tiptoed out of the room.
Still crying, Tom hugged the bear with all his might.
"Listen, Tom," the teddy bear suddenly whispered in his ear.
"I want to tell you a story."
So Tom listened.

There was once a small bear who lived with his mother in a cave.
Every morning, Mother Bear woke Little Bear
and they went out together into the forest.
Mother Bear looked for food with Little Bear, and she showed
him which things were good to eat and which were not.
They played catch or hide-and-seek together, and Mother Bear
let him climb a little and splash around in the stream.

But sometimes Mother Bear
had work to do—cleaning out the cave
or gathering fresh branches for their bed.
It was boring for Little Bear, and it
made him grumpy. And he didn't cheer up
until Mother Bear was ready to play again.

Every night she licked him with her pink tongue, from the tips of his fluffy ears right down to the last claw on his little hind leg. Then with a happy growl she murmured, "Sleep well, and sweet dreams, Little Bear," and she laid him down on a fragrant bed of soft pine branches. Then they slept, snuggled close together, all through the night.

But the best thing of all was when Father Bear came. He picked up
Little Bear in his huge paws and threw him high in the air until he
squealed like a piglet.

Then they went out together, deep into the forest, and Father Bear
showed Little Bear animals that he never saw when he played with
Mother near the cave.

They saw the old badger in his burrow, and he growled at them.
But Father Bear growled back, and that was the end of that.

High on the cliffs, they saw the sly lynx, watching for prey.
And above the cliffs they could see the great eagle, circling in
the blue sky.

Father Bear let Little Bear climb much higher in the trees than Mother ever did, and balancing on the shaky limbs was an adventure. When Little Bear was hungry, Father Bear scooped a fat fish from the river with one swish of his paw. And for dessert, Father Bear broke open a bees' nest. Delicious! After eating, they played rough and tumble until—at last!—Little Bear pushed his father onto his back. His father pretended to be beaten, and they both laughed and laughed and rolled down a hillside. Then they lay together all calm and happy in the meadow and let the sun warm their fur.

But when evening came, Father Bear took Little Bear back home.

Little Bear plunked down in the
opening of the cave, folded his arms, and scowled.
Father Bear dusted him off and picked a blade of grass out
of his fur—but Little Bear made a face and turned away.
So Father Bear lumbered off into the forest.
Mother Bear watched from the shadows, and then came
and tried to cheer Little Bear up. But he bellowed and
scratched the ground and didn't want to cheer up.
Then he started to whimper.

Mother Bear let him whimper for a little while. Then she padded over
to the bed of branches and fetched him the ball of soft moss he liked
to hug. She gently put it in Little Bear's paws, and sat next to him.

"Why is he going away again?" wept Little Bear.

"Because Father Bear lives in his own cave now," said Mother Bear softly.

"But he used to live here!" sobbed Little Bear.

"Yes, that was when Father Bear and I still liked to be with each other.
But then we started arguing. You remember. And it isn't good to
live with someone if you're always arguing," said Mother Bear.

Little Bear thought about that.

He thought about the animals he met in the forest. Some were friendly,
and they would play together for hours. But he argued with some
of the other animals—he didn't like being with them so much.

"But *I* didn't quarrel with Daddy Bear," growled Little Bear.
"That's true, Little Bear, and that's why Daddy Bear comes so often
to take you out to play. You are his child and you always will be.
He loves you more than anyone else."

Little Bear yawned. "When is Daddy coming back?"
"Soon, Little Bear. Very soon."

"Next time I'll wave good-bye to him," said Little Bear, and
he rolled sleepily onto his back. "And I'll give him a giant
bear hug, and I'll shout, 'Good-bye, Daddy!'"

"That will make us all happy," Mother Bear whispered,
but Little Bear was already fast asleep.

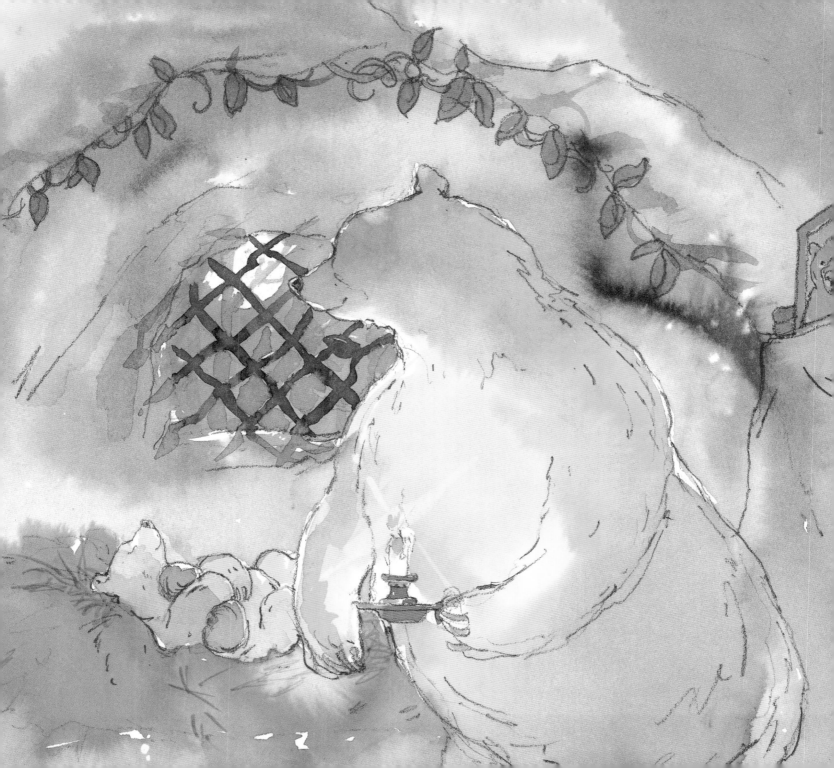

When teddy finished telling the story, Tom was almost asleep.
So teddy bear closed his eyes too, and he whispered, "Good night, Tom."
And Tom murmured, "Good night, bear. Sleep well, and sweet dreams."

Copyright © 1995 by Michael Neugebauer Verlag AG, Gossau Zürich, Switzerland.
First published in Switzerland under the title *Auf Wiedersehen, Papa!*
English translation copyright © 1995 by North-South Books Inc.

First published in the United States, Canada, Great Britain, Australia, and
New Zealand in 1995 by North-South Books, an imprint of Nord-Süd Verlag AG,
Gossau Zürich, Switzerland. First paperback edition published in 1997.

Library of Congress Cataloging-in-Publication Data
Weninger, Brigitte.
[Auf Wiedersehen, Papa! English]
Good-bye, daddy! / Brigitte Weninger ; illustrated by Alan Marks.
"A Michael Neugebauer book."
Summary: A little boy's teddy bear helps him come to terms with his parents'
divorce by telling him a story about a little bear in similar circumstances.
[1. Divorce—Fiction. 2. Parent and child—Fiction. 3. Teddy bears—Fiction.]
I. Marks, Alan, ill. II. Title
PZ7.W46916Go l995 [Fic]—dc20 94-35490

A CIP catalogue record for this book is available
from The British Library.

ISBN 1-55858-383-1 (trade binding)
1 2 3 4 5 6 7 8 9 10
ISBN 1-55858-384-X (library binding)
1 2 3 4 5 6 7 8 9 10
ISBN 1-55858-770-5 (paperback)
1 2 3 4 5 6 7 8 9 10
Printed in Belgium

For more information about our
books, and the authors and artists
who create them, visit our web site:
http://www.northsouth.com